# Dunkin' Dazza's Dribble

ANDREW EINSPRUCH

*Illustrated by Peter Foster*

SupaDooPers

sundance
A Haights Cross Communications Company

Published by
Sundance Publishing
234 Taylor Street
Littleton, MA 01460

Copyright © text Andrew Einspruch
Copyright © illustrations Peter Foster
Project commissioned and managed by
Lorraine Bambrough-Kelly, The Writer's Style
Designed by Cath Lindsey/design rescue

First published 1998 by
Addison Wesley Longman Australia Pty Limited
95 Coventry Street
South Melbourne 3205 Australia
Exclusive United States Distribution: Sundance Publishing

ISBN 0-7608-3290-0

Printed In Canada

# CONTENTS

*To Billie*
*For love, support, and red ink*

# CHAPTER 1

# Don't Mess With a Garbage Truck

Choko looked like a truck had hit him.

"What happened?" I asked.

"A truck hit me."

"Ouch."

"Yeah. Don't try it."

His voice sounded like gravel. He was putting on a brave face, but he wasn't fooling anyone.

"I was on my bike, looking right. I should've looked left. I rode in front of a garbage truck. I don't remember much, but I guess I landed on my back."

A nurse poked a needle the size of a submarine into his arm. "This young man's lucky to be alive."

"They keep doing tests, X-rays, MRIs . . ."
Choko winced and the brave face cracked.
"I . . . I . . . " His face lost the fight against
tears. "I don't know if I'm gonna walk
again."

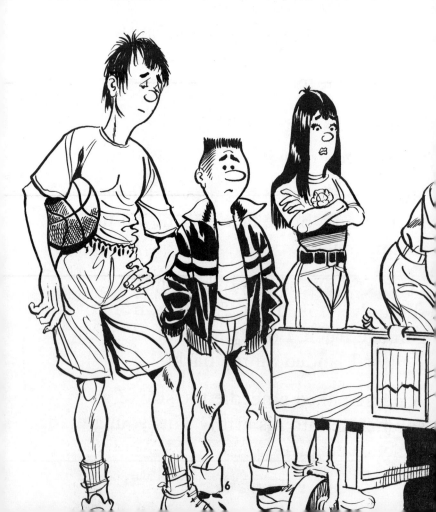

When we first heard the news, Darrin "Dunkin' Dazza" Bowman and I were three points behind at two-on-two against his sister, Ellen, and her friend, Cat. We dropped everything, sprinted for the hospital, and found my best friend looking like an extra in a gangster movie.

Ellen touched Choko's hand. "Just wait, Chokoid. You'll be swishing three-pointers in no time."

He sniffed and swallowed. "Know what's really stupid? The doctors told my parents that therapy and everything will cost over a hundred thousand dollars. There's no way my folks can pay that."

"Don't think about it," Darrin said. "Just get better."

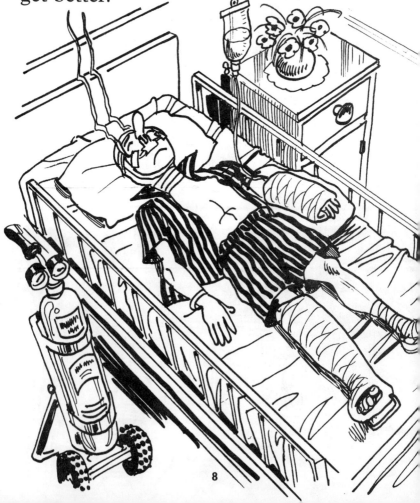

Silence filled the room like the lump filling my throat. All you could hear was the electronic beep of that gadget that tells you if you're still alive.

"Gosh, he's a mess," I said, as we left the hospital. "We've got to do something."

"Maybe we could help with money," said Darrin.

"Sure." Ellen flung an arm around her brother's shoulder. "Got a spare thousand?"

Cat's eyes lit up. "We could raise it."

The hospital staff said Choko would start therapy in a month. We could barely scrape together enough for a burger, so raising thousands seemed as easy as growing a third arm. But Choko's pasty face and fractured spine were fresh in our minds.

"We've got four weeks," I said. "Let's get cracking."

# CHAPTER 2

# $22.95

"How long have we been here?" I asked Darrin.

"Four hours and thirty-seven minutes."

"I feel like a moron."

We'd set up a table on Main Street. Most of the cookies and muffins we'd baked were still there half a day later. And from the number of things that were half-burned, you could tell we spent more time on basketball courts than in kitchens.

"Pretty sad effort."

Darrin nodded. "$7.95."

"How long have we been here?" I asked Darrin.

"Three hours and forty-six minutes."

"Maybe we should put up more Car Wash signs."

"Hey, we've almost doubled yesterday's earnings," said Cat. "Fifteen bucks."

I dropped my rag in a bucket. "This stinks."

"So *you* do better."

"How long have we been here?" I asked Darrin.

"Twenty minutes."

"Seems like an eternity."

I held my accordion and bowed, as an old man dropped 10 cents in my hat. The old guy must have been deaf, because everyone else grimaced and raced past us.

Ellen snorted. "Choko will be in an old folks home before we raise $150."

"Yeah," said Darrin. "We're shooting too low."

13

"That's it!" Everyone looked at Ellen. "What we know is basketball, right? So we'll put on a Hoopathon."

"I'm with you, Ellen," Darrin said. "We put on a tournament, and everyone gets sponsors to donate money for each basket they score."

My accordion wheezed to a halt. "It's gotta be better than playing music on the street."

"If it's one-on-one instead of teams of five," piped in Cat, "it'll be easier to get people to play."

That was it. The Hoopathon was on.

# CHAPTER 3

# Burritos and Pizza

We picked a Saturday.

Cat and Ellen painted dozens of posters, and printed sponsor sheets on the computer. Darrin and I booked referees and the gym.

With a week to go, we met at my place for burritos.

Ellen walked in and threw down her hat. "I can't believe we've got another flop on our hands."

"Don't say that," protested Cat. "I've got sponsors. Five bucks a point."

Darrin grabbed some paper. "So who's got what?"

Everyone mumbled a number.

"That's $12.00 a point between all of us. Plus, seven other people who are supposed to show up."

I scooped up a glob of refried beans and cheese. "We need more like $40 a point, or it *will* be a flop."

Ellen pushed her plate aside. "We're not trying hard enough."

"Yeah," said Darrin. "We've gotta ask everyone—businesspeople, strangers—everyone."

"I hate doing that sort of thing," I said, shoving down another bite. I'd rather staple my foot to the floor than talk to people I don't know.

"Yeah, well, Choko doesn't seem too fond of what he's doing right now, either."

I stopped eating.

"How is he?" asked Cat.

Ellen shrugged. "He still has no feeling in his legs. Tomorrow they do something gross with his spinal fluid."

The room got quiet.

"I think I know some other people I can ask," I whispered.

Darrin, Ellen, and I spent the next morning talking to store managers at the mall.

"How are you doin'?" asked Darrin.

"Not much better," I said. "$15.50 a point."

"Anyone tried Julio Piotsa?" asked Ellen.

Julio owned the Piotsa's Pizza chain. He wasn't just a basketball nut. He was a king-sized, raving basketball pistachio, especially with his son, Al "Tree Top" Piotsa, about to go pro. And thanks to Julio's Fabulous Deep Pan Secret Sauce Pizzas, he was a rich nut, too.

"So, kids, what can I get you?" Julio towered over the counter. You could see where Tree Top got his height.

I stuttered into my Hoopathon routine. He listened patiently, but I could tell from his eyes that I wasn't getting anywhere.

"Tell you what," he said. "Seeing that it's basketball, each of you can put me down for a dollar a point, and you can put posters in the window."

We thanked him and dragged ourselves out of the pizzeria.

21

Darrin tried to put a good spin on it. "Better than nothing."

"Barely," I muttered.

Ellen stopped. "Look."

Looming like a T-rex above the crowd was Tree Top Piotsa.

"Let's ask him," she whispered.

"What? To sponsor us?"

"No. To play," Ellen said.

I tried to fake confidence. "Uh,
Mr. Piotsa?"

He stopped. "Tree Top will do."

"Right. Tree Top. Anyway, I was wondering,
um, if you might, uh, we have this, y'know,
Hoopathon, and uh . . . "

"Hoopathon?" He peered down at me like a half-amused giraffe.

"Yeah, I mean, we, there's . . . " My brain shut down, and my tongue went numb. I just couldn't do it. I felt like I was asking the President to come to a pajama party.

And then I thought of Choko lying facedown with a needle stuck in his back. I had to ask.

Tree Top actually heard me out. "So your friend can't walk?"

"It's not looking good."

"Well, I've played a lot of basketball, but never in a Hoopathon. Sounds like fun. Count me in."

"You're kidding! I mean, great!"

# CHAPTER 4

# A Wrong Guess

That night, Darrin and Ellen played one-on-one in my backyard. Ellen didn't quite have Darrin's size, but she was quick and had her brother's nose for the hoop. She was up by three.

As usual, they played like the future of western civilization was at stake. They didn't joke. They barely spoke. Tension hung over their strictly-business session.

The phone rang. It was Tree Top Piotsa. "I thought I'd tell you—my dad's sponsoring me for $80 a point. And I managed to get him to do the same for you and your teammates."

"Fantastic!"

"And he's put up $1000 for the winner. I thought that might help."

I slammed down the phone and whooped.

With a name like Piotsa involved, people would take us seriously. On Friday night, we guessed there would be 65 players on Saturday.

We guessed wrong. Very wrong.

We arrived to set up at 7:00 A.M. and found a dozen guys waiting. By nine o'clock there were 176, including Tree Top and some friends, plus twice as many spectators.

"This is a nightmare," said Ellen. "Even with six baskets, we'll be here until the next moon landing."

I nodded. "We'll never get through the first round, much less the finals."

"People are getting restless," said Cat. "We've got to start."

"How about dividing everyone up into groups and playing two-on-two?" said Darrin.

I tapped the microphone. "Excuse me."
Everyone kept shooting and yakking, so
Ellen shrieked a window-shattering whistle.

Silence.

I looked out over the sea of T-shirts and
shorts, cleared the nervousness from my
throat, and launched into a welcome.
"We're gonna have to play two-on-two," I
explained. "Games will be on half-courts.
Each basket is one point. First pair to get
21 points wins, but they have to win by two."

Minutes later, a referee pulled the first two slips of paper from a bucket—Ellen Bowman, Al Piotsa.

Ellen and Tree Top. That was gonna be a tough team.

The rest of the names were pulled out, until there were only two left in the bucket.

Mine. And Darrin's.

"Looks like you're stuck with me," I said.

"We'll do fine," Darrin said, as he smiled.

# CHAPTER 5

# Hard Work

Round-robin groups whittled the 88 pairs down to 16.

Tree Top and Ellen charged forward to the head of their group.

Darrin and I were slower. We coughed and spluttered and played our hearts out. Riding on Darrin's five-star performance, we scraped to the top of our group, too.

Cat made the cut with Tree Top's friend, Sledge Andrews.

By lunch, my nerves were shot, and my body felt like it had spent a week as a tackling dummy.

Tree Top, eyes glowing, joined us with Ellen. "This much hoops is a total gas," he said.

Ellen eyed her brother. "You look beat."

"I've had easier days, but we're getting there. Ozone's playing well."

He meant I hadn't screwed up—too often.

Cat jogged over with a calculator. "Look."

"19,627," I read.

"Now add the word 'dollars.' That's what we've raised already, and there are still the fifteen play-off games."

# CHAPTER 6

# Phew!

We were up 20–19 in the semifinals when the world went black.

"Look at my face," said Darrin. "Focus on me."

"I can't breathe," I gasped.

"You got the wind knocked out of you."

"Now I know why they call him 'Sledge.'"

We had to win this game in order to advance to the finals—where Ellen and Tree Top were waiting.

This game made the morning game feel like a seaside stroll. Every muscle begged for mercy as I gasped for air.

Cat came over. "You okay, Ozo? You need anything?"

"I'll manage. Maybe you can lend me your lungs for a while."

It was my foul shot. I struggled to my feet and tried to force the two images of the basket back together. Stars danced in front of my eyes.

I knew why I hated free throws. It's lonely at the foul line. There's always pressure. Everyone's attention is focused on you—and I miss 9 times out of 10.

Darrin saw my eyes glazing over. "The basket, Ozone. Aim for the square on the backboard."

Weird. Usually he says to go for a swish.

"Sink it for Choko."

The gym was silent, waiting. I cleared my head and let the ball fly for the painted square.

It bounced in. We were in the finals!

# CHAPTER 7

# Up Against a Tree

We had a twenty-minute rest. I sat and tried to pretend it was a week. My gut burned, and I felt like I was going to be sick.

Too soon, the finalists were introduced. Us.

Julio Piotsa waved for the microphone.
"I want to congratulate everyone here for a
splendid effort. Perhaps you'll all join me in
digging deeper. For this game, I pledge
$500 for every point."

The crowed cheered, and the game was on.

Obviously, Darrin had to take on Tree Top, which left me covering Ellen—hard enough on a good day, let alone now.

Tree Top popped in three quick points, one straight over the top of Darrin's head.

When we got the ball again, Darrin grabbed my arm. "His rebounding could be better," he murmured. "Start taking longer shots. I'll scoop up whatever you miss."

My first shot fell way short, but Darrin made it look like a perfect assist and sank one.

My next attempt hit the rim and bounced to Darrin. Another point.

Then this feeling came over me. You hear about runners "hitting the wall," where they pass through exhaustion, then get a new burst of energy. That must be what happened to me. I couldn't shake the feeling that, somehow, Choko was watching, and there was no way I was gonna slack off.

I knew I had to contain Ellen—so I just did it! I batted at passes, blocked shots, and stayed in her face. It made a difference. Darrin and I pulled the game even at 16, and stayed even up to 20 all.

Then it was pretty much sudden death. The first two-point lead would win.

It didn't happen. Every basket was answered immediately. Darrin and Tree Top got rough under the basket. Elbows flew, as both constantly pushed the other, trying for an advantage. 25 all. 30 all.

At 35 all, Darrin said to me, "You take Tree Top."

"Have you lost it?" I asked.

"We have to try something different. Crowd him like you did Ellen."

Me covering Tree Top was stupid, but it confused him. Instead of blasting past like he should have, he planted himself and tried to figure out what was going on.

That was mistake number one. It let me knock the ball out of his hands, to Darrin. Dunkin' Dazza shot to half-court, turned, and zipped past Ellen for a lay-up.

We were up by one!

Ellen took the ball this time and passed it to Tree Top, who heaved it back.

That was mistake number two. Ellen tried to set up a play, but Darrin screened her like an eclipse. She dumped off a wild pass, and Tree Top and I scrambled after it. The ball skittered out of bounds.

Tree Top had touched it last. Our ball.

I fired a short bounce pass to Darrin, then raced toward the basket. Tree Top didn't have time to swap defense with Ellen. He had to come after me.

Darrin crouched face-to-face against his sister. It was like watching them in my backyard. They had their Future-of-the-Universe-Hangs-in-the-Balance looks.

He dribbled fast and low. The ball flashed left and right behind his back. Darrin teased his sister with it. She swatted at the ball again and again, but missed. Her face was a mask of fury. Ellen and Darrin looked like they were ready to kill each other.

Then Darrin did something I'd never seen him do, even goofing around. He dribbled the ball through Ellen's legs and past her. He dribbled it so hard, it sailed up toward the basket on the bounce.

Darrin flew after it. He met the ball at the rim and stuffed it through.

Our game! The crowd went wild.

"Pretty spectacular, Darro." Ellen gave Darrin a quick hug.

"Thanks."

"But next time, I'll be ready."

Cat was at the mike. " . . . thanks to all of you—and with a special thank you to Mr. Piotsa—we've raised $72,143.21 for Choko!"

Choko's dad stood at the mike, tears streaming down his face. "On behalf of my son and my wife, I want to thank everyone here. This means so much to us.

I also want to let you all know that . . ."

His voice cracked, and he wiped his eyes. "Today we received the results of Choko's latest tests. The damage to my son's spine is not permanent. With your help, he'll walk again."

Everyone stood and cheered wildly.

It went on and on and on.

I felt like crying. In fact, I did.

Choko was gonna be all right!

*Andrew Einspruch*

As a kid, Andrew Einspruch used to play one-on-one with his friend Kent. But unlike Ozone and Darrin, he never won a Hoopathon.

Andrew has written everything from computer manuals to song parodies, but he prefers to write fiction for younger readers.

He lives with his writer wife, Billie Dean, and when he's not at his desk, he's running after their daughter, their dogs, or their horses—often all at the same time!

*Peter Foster*

Peter has loved to draw for as long as he can remember. When he was four years old, he got into trouble for drawing a canoe on the living room wall with his sister's lipstick! In high school, his math teacher was unhappy to find Peter drawing comic strip characters in the back of his math book.

As an adult, Peter has taught art in high school and has worked for advertising agencies. Currently, he illustrates children's books and draws an adventure comic strip for the Sunday edition of a newspaper.

When he's not drawing, Peter loves to play the piano and write songs. He also loves boats, beaches, and warm sea breezes.